For Emily.

Once upon a time there was a little white rabbit called Juggi who lived with her mum, dad and three brothers in the woods.

Juggi was a lively rabbit. She always wanted to explore new places and kept wandering off and getting lost.

Her mother kept telling Juggi to be careful and not to wander too far from home. She told her to always remember that if she got lost they lived near the biggest oak tree in the forest.

One day Juggi was playing with her brothers when she decided she was bored. She wanted to see what was happening in the big world outside the forest so she wandered off into the town.

All of the big buildings and all of the noise that came from the cars and buses puzzled Juggi. She started to feel scared so she decided to go back home.

Juggi looked around to find the tall oak tree that her mother had told her about but all she could see was tall buildings and long roads. Poor Juggi was lost and she felt very scared. She wanted to get back to her family but did not know which way to go.

Juggi was so afraid she ran and entered the first doorway she saw. Juggi did not know that it was a doorway to a paint shop. She entered the shop and hid between the tins of paint.

All of a sudden, Juggi heard footsteps. Someone was coming into the shop. She panicked, leapt in the air and hopped towards the door. As she did, Juggi knocked over a tin of blue paint. The paint spilled all over her soft white fur, turning it blue.

Juggi did not know that she was now a blue rabbit. She still thought she was a white rabbit.

Juggi ran out of the paint shop as fast as she could and hopped down the street. Tired, and out of breath, Juggi stopped in front of another doorway where there was a mirrored door. Juggi saw a blue rabbit looking back at her.

She had never seen a mirror before and did not know that it was just her reflection. Juggi was delighted to see another rabbit. Juggi thought that she had made a new friend.

She hopped up to the mirror and the blue rabbit also hopped up to the mirror. When Juggi ran back and forth in front of the mirror, the blue rabbit copied her.

Whatever Juggi did, the blue rabbit did the same. Then she finally realised that it was not a new friend she had made, but she was seeing an image of herself in the mirror. Worse still, she had turned into a blue rabbit!

Juggi felt so lonely and frightened and she started to cry. She was all alone in the big, busy town and she worried that she would not be able see her family ever again. Juggi started to panic. She stood up tall and thumped her back legs.

Suddenly, she felt a gentle hand stroke her ears and Juggi felt at ease.

The hand belonged to a little girl, who cuddled Juggi and said, "Don't be afraid. My name is Emily. You are a beautiful blue rabbit and I will look after you. I will be your friend."

Juggi was so happy and felt safe and secure as Emily cuddled her. Emily said to Juggi, "I will bring you home with me and you can meet my ginger cat called Dexter."

Emily wondered what name she should give to her new friend. "I cannot keep calling you Blue Rabbit," Emily told her. "I will have to think of a name. I will ask Grandad to help."

Emily brought Juggi home to meet Dexter and they became the best of friends. They would play together and chase each other around the garden. Sometimes Dexter would run upstairs and lie on Emily's bed. Juggi would follow him but Emily would shout, "No, no, no! Rabbits and cats are not allowed on the bed."

One day Emily asked Grandad to help her pick a name for her blue rabbit. Grandad said, "The blue rabbit's ears are just like jugs so let's call her Juggi."

Juggi was very happy living in Emily's house, playing with Dexter and being cuddled by Emily, but sometimes she was sad when she thought about her mum, dad and three brothers living in the forest.

Juggi missed her real family and wanted to go home. Juggi knew that Emily was a lovely, kind girl and would help her to get home to the forest if only she could tell her about her family. But Juggi could not talk so how could she explain this to Emily?

One day, Emily was reading a book about white rabbits in the forest. When Juggi saw the pictures of rabbits and trees she jumped up and down excitedly.

She wanted to show Emily that her family looked like those white rabbits; indeed they were not blue rabbits. Emily looked at Juggi and knew that she was upset.

She realised that she was missing her rabbit family. Emily really loved Juggi but knew that Juggi should be with her real family. No matter how much she would miss Juggi, her beautiful blue rabbit, she wanted Juggi to be happy.

Emily asked her mum and dad to help her find the forest and search for Juggi's family. They agreed to help, so one day they set off to search for the forest where Juggi's family lived.

Juggi was sad to say goodbye to Dexter but was excited to look for her real family. Dexter looked out the window and gloomily waved goodbye to his new friend. Who would have thought that a ginger cat and a blue rabbit could have been such good friends?

When Emily arrived at the forest with her mum and dad, Juggi jumped out of the car and excitedly hopped around. Juggi could see the forest and the big oak tree her mother had told her about, "if you ever get lost look for the biggest oak tree and that is where your family live." Juggi knew she was home so all she had to do was find her family.

Juggi and Emily ran towards the big oak tree and Juggi saw her mum, her dad and her three brothers playing around the tree. Juggi hopped up to them shouting, "I'm home! I'm home!"

She was surprised when they did not know her. Then she remembered that she was no longer the white rabbit that they had always known, but she was now a blue rabbit. Her family did not recognise her.

Juggi started to cry. Then all of a sudden it started to rain. Emily felt sad as she watched Juggi crying in the rain but as the rain got heavier something strange was happening.

The ground around Juggi was turning blue. The blue paint was washing off from Juggi's blue fur and now she had her snow white colour back.

Now Juggi's family recognised her and ran to greet her. They leapt in the air and kissed and cuddled their missing rabbit. Emily was sad to say goodbye to Juggi but knew it was best for Juggi to be with her own family. She knew it would be selfish to keep Juggi all to herself.

Emily would never forget her blue rabbit.